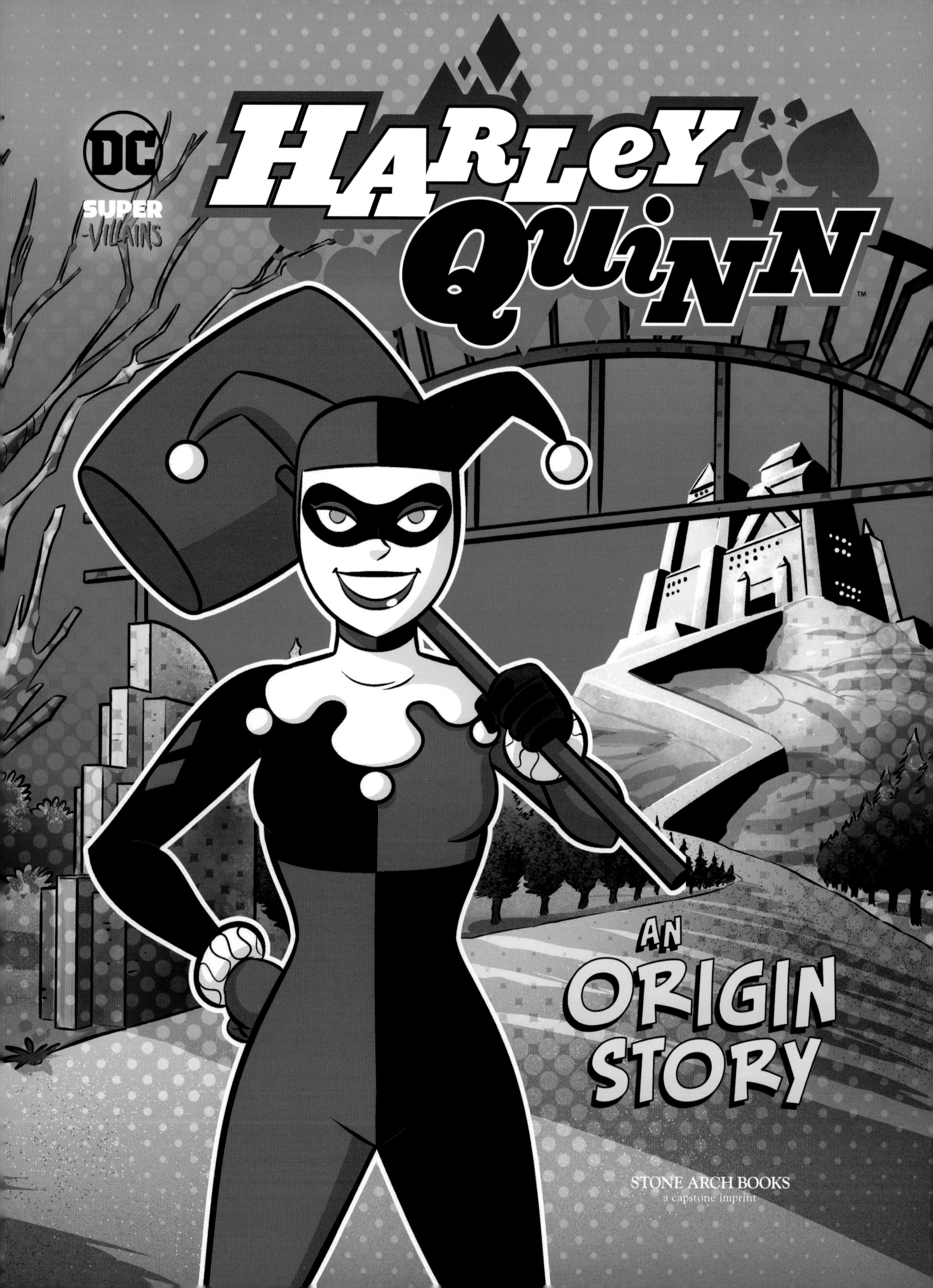
DC
SUPER-VILLAINS
HARLEY QUINN™
AN ORIGIN STORY
STONE ARCH BOOKS
a capstone imprint

Published by Stone Arch Books, an imprint of Capstone
1710 Roe Crest Drive, North Mankato, Minnesota 56003
capstonepub.com

Cataloging-in-Publication Data is available on the Library of Congress website.

ISBN: 9781666345285 (hardcover)
ISBN: 9781666345339 (paperback)
ISBN: 9781666345322 (ebook PDF)

Summary: How did Harley Quinn become Batman's jolly jester enemy? Discover the story behind
this Super-Villain's journey from promising psychologist to Clown Princess of Crime.

Contributing artists: Erik Doescher, Tim Levins, and Luciano Vecchio

Designed by Hilary Wacholz

SUPER
-VILLAINS

AN ORIGIN STORY

WRITTEN BY
LAURIE S. SUTTON

ILLUSTRATED BY
DARIO BRIZUELA

BATMAN CREATED BY
BOB KANE WITH BILL FINGER

Today is Dr. Harleen Quinzel's first day of work at Arkham Asylum. This place is a special prison for Super-Villains. Her job is to help the prisoners with their mental health.

4

Dr. Quinzel walks down the hall of cells.

The Riddler, the Penguin, Poison Ivy! Each one has a story about what made them into Super-Villains, she thinks. I want to learn all about them.

Dr. Quinzel stops in front of a cell.

But mostly I want to know more about the Joker! she thinks.

She rubs her chin. *There has to be a reason why he uses dangerous gags to commit crimes. He has a clown's face, but he is a serious villain.*

Dr. Quinzel talks to the Joker during therapy sessions. He tells her about his life growing up. It's a sad story. She feels sorry for him.

What she doesn't know is that the Joker is lying. It's all a joke to him. But to Dr. Quinzel, it's very serious.

The Joker is just misunderstood, she thinks. *Batman is the real bad guy!*

Her feelings of sympathy turn into a crazy kind of love.

Then one day, the Joker escapes.

He battles Batman in Gotham City.

Dr. Quinzel reads all about it in the newspapers. She laughs at the Joker's tricks.

It sounds like he's having a hoot! she thinks.

But soon Batman brings the Joker back to Arkham. Dr. Quinzel is furious that the Dark Knight has caught her secret sweetheart.

My poor angel! she thinks. *That grouch Batman ruined all his fun!*

Dr. Quinzel knows what she has to do. That night, she robs a novelty store. She snatches a clownlike harlequin costume. She grabs some toys and gimmicks.

Dr. Quinzel puts on the black and red costume. She sneaks back into Arkham Asylum. She sticks explosives onto a joke alarm clock.

She blows open the Joker's cell.

"Knock, knock, Puddin'!" she tells the Joker. "You're a free clown now!"

On that night, Harleen Quinzel becomes Harley Quinn!

Harley Quinn is the opposite of
Dr. Harleen Quinzel. The doctor was
serious. The Super-Villain is wild.

Harley uses gags like
a giant circus mallet
and stink bombs.
But they're no joke.
They pack a
real punch!

Harley also has amazing gymnastic skills. She can flip and jump like a circus acrobat.

After busting the Joker out of
Arkham, Harley Quinn sticks with
her sweetie. She becomes his sidekick.
She calls him Puddin' and Mr. J.

On her first crime with the Joker, Harley helps him try to grab Police Commissioner Gordon at an awards ceremony. Batman spoils the plot, but the villains escape to their hideout.

Another time, the Joker and Harley set a trap for Commissioner Gordon at his dentist's office.

"Hey, Commish!" Harley says. "You can have a smile just like Mr. J. All you need is some great dental care!"

Just in time, Batman crashes through the window. He rescues his friend from the criminal clowns.

The crooks escape again. Except this time, the Joker is mad.

"I don't know how, but you messed up my perfect plan!" the Joker yells at Harley.

"I'm sorry, Mr. J," Harley replies. "I don't know how I messed it up either."

The Joker blames Harley for the failed plots. He's so mad that he kicks her out of their hideout.

"I'll show him!" Harley says. "I'll do a big robbery on my own. Then *I'll* be the one who's laughing. *HA!*"

Harley decides to steal a rare diamond from a museum. She uses her gymnastic skills to leap around the security lasers.

FWIP! FWIP!

She gets by without setting

off any alarms.

WHEE-OOO! WHEE-OOO!

Suddenly the alarms go off!
But Harley isn't the one who did it.

Poison Ivy runs by. She's robbing
the place too! She's stealing plant
toxins from the museum's lab.

"Hey! Plant-controlling lady!"
Harley shouts. "The idea is to *not*
set off the alarms."

But the alarms keep ringing.

Squads of police arrive.

Harley and Ivy run for the exit together, but the police chase them. Then Harley has a crazy idea. She grabs a bottle of plant toxin from Ivy.

"Heads up!" Harley yells as she throws the bottle.

SMAAAASH!

The bottle breaks. A cloud of green gas leaks out.

Harley and Ivy run past the coughing police officers. They dash out of the museum and jump into Poison Ivy's getaway car.

ZOOOOM!

They speed down the street.

"This could be the beginning of a beautiful friendship!" Poison Ivy says.

Harley and Ivy team up again after that. They rob a club for men only—no women allowed. The men are shocked when the female felons burst into their meeting.

"What is the meaning of this?" one man yells.

Harley and Ivy don't listen to the grumbling. Instead, Harley drops two large seedpods.

PLOP! PLOP!

Poison Ivy uses her power. Huge vines burst from the pods. The plants wrap around the men.

WHOOOSH! WHOOOSH!

"That'll keep you busy while we rob your trophy room," Poison Ivy says.

Harley laughs. "This is fun! I sure am glad I met you, Ivy!"

Harley Quinn and Poison Ivy keep up their crooked fun. They go on to steal priceless plants. They rob a jewelry store. Soon, the newspapers call them the New Queens of Crime.

The pair become best friends.

Harley Quinn spreads her own kind of chaos all over Gotham City.

She stops being the Joker's sidekick. She becomes a Super-Villain in her own right. Harley earns the name Clown Princess of Crime.

Everyone says that Harley has a crazy sense of humor. But she's just trying to have a little fun . . . and a good laugh!

41

HARLEY QUINN™

REAL NAME: DR. HARLEEN QUINZEL
CRIMINAL NAME: HARLEY QUINN
ROLE: SUPER-VILLAIN
BASE: GOTHAM CITY

Harley Quinn has a crazy sense of humor. She uses a huge circus mallet, laughing gas, and other gags to carry out her crimes. Harley acts like a clown, but she's a serious Super-Villain. She just wants to have a little fun . . . and have a good laugh when the joke's on Batman!

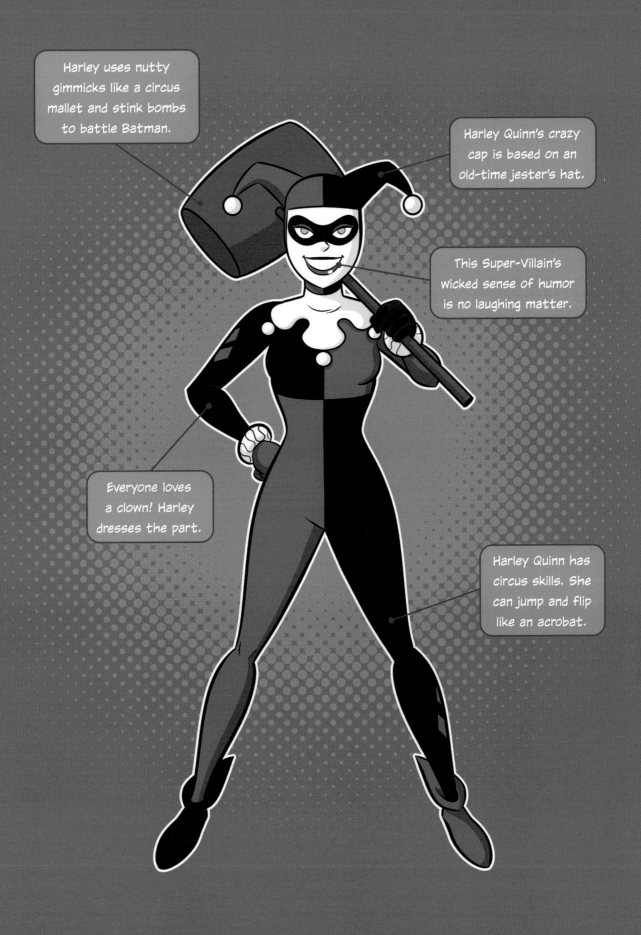

THE AUTHOR

LAURIE S. SUTTON has been reading comics since she was a kid. She grew up to become an editor for Marvel, DC Comics, Starblaze, and Tekno Comics. She has written Adam Strange for DC, Star Trek: Voyager for Marvel, plus Star Trek: Deep Space Nine and Witch Hunter for Malibu Comics. There are long boxes of comics in her closet where there should be clothing and shoes. Laurie has lived all over the world and currently resides in Florida.

THE ILLUSTRATOR

DARIO BRIZUELA works traditionally and digitally in many different illustration styles. His work can be found in a wide range of properties, including Star Wars Tales, DC Super Hero Girls, DC Super Friends, Transformers, Scooby-Doo! Team-Up and more. Brizuela lives in Buenos Aires, Argentina.

GLOSSARY

acrobat (AK-ruh-bat)—a person skilled at tumbling, balancing, and other gymnastic acts

gimmick (GIM-ik)—a special or hidden device used to pull tricks

harlequin (HAR-luh-kwin)—a character in old stories who acts silly and wears a mask and diamond-patterned clothes

mallet (MA-let)—a hammerlike tool with a long handle and a barrel-shaped head on its end

novelty (NOV-uhl-tee)—a toy, ornament, or other item that is bought for fun

sympathy (SIM-puh-thee)—feeling sorry for another person and the troubles they are facing

therapy (THER-uh-pee)—the treatment of mental illness by talking with someone trained to listen and help

toxin (TOK-sin)—poison made by a living thing

DISCUSSION QUESTIONS

Write down your answers. Look back at the story for help.

QUESTION 1.

Do you think Harley Quinn is good, evil, or both? Why? Use examples from the story to explain your answer.

QUESTION 2.

How do you think Harley felt when the Joker kicked her out of their hideout? What makes you think that?

QUESTION 3.

Harley and Ivy like to team up. What makes a good teammate? If you could work with any Super Hero or Super-Villain, who would you pick?

QUESTION 4.

What is your favorite illustration in this book? Explain why you made your choice.

READ THEM ALL!!

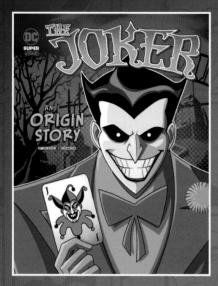

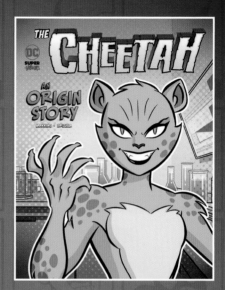

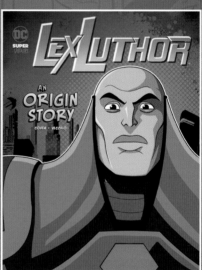

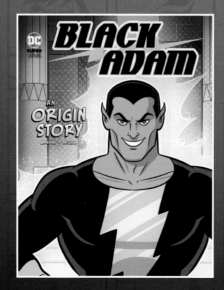